THE TOTALLY NINJA RACCOONS MEET THE LITTLE GREEN MEN

by Kevin Coolidge

Illustrated by Jubal Lee

Be a reading ninja!

Kevin Coolidge

The Totally Ninja Raccoons Are:

Rascal:
He's the shortest brother and loves doughnuts. He's great with his paws and makes really cool gadgets. He's a little goofy and loves both his brothers, even when they pick on him, but maybe not right then.

Bandit:
He's the oldest brother. He's tall and lean. He's super smart and loves to read. He leads the Totally Ninja Raccoons, but he couldn't do it by himself.

Kevin:
He may be the middle brother, but he refuses to be stuck in the middle. He has the moves and the street smarts that the Totally Ninja Raccoons are going to need, even if it does sometimes get them into trouble as well as out of trouble.

CONTENTS

1. A Bright Idea   page 1

2. A Shower of Stars   page 7

3. Unidentified Flying Objects   page 13

4. Is Being Green Mean?   page 17

5. The Trap is Sprung   page 23

6. Asking for Help   page 27

7. Spring to Action   page 33

8. What Do Unicorns Eat?   page 41

"We place several high intensity lights at dumpster, and when the raccoons come..."

1

A BRIGHT IDEA

It's a beautiful night in Wellsboro, Pennsylvania. The skies are clear. The stars twinkle. The Cat Board once again plots against the Totally Ninja Raccoons.

A plump calico cat sits up straight. It's Gypsy, head of the Cat Board. "This meeting will now come to order," meows Gypsy.

A black and white tuxedo cat perks up his ears and laughs. "More like odor. Finn farted!"

An all-black cat, black as a moonless night, snarls, "I did not fart!"

A pure white Persian cat sniffs, waves her paw around, and looks embarrassed. "Meow, pardon me, my fellow felines. I'm on a special seafood diet. It is NOT flatulence. It's the wind whispering, and I think it smells delightful."

"It sounds like your butt is shouting to me. I can hear it from over here," chuckles Huck, "and it's stink-ee, pee-yew!"

"Hey, I'm on the 'see food' diet, too! If I see it, I eat it!" laughs Finn.

A sleek and beautiful Siamese cat holds her delicate paw over her nose. "You are definitely NOT a unicorn with a stench like that!"

Gypsy glares. "That is quite enough about farts, unicorns, and diets. We have important business to discuss."

A nearly hairless cat mews softly. It is a Sphinx cat. "I'm here to propose a solution to our number one problem."

"Finn farting?" meows Huck.

"No, the Totally Ninja Raccoons!" growls Gyspy. "Now, tell me about this final fix for those pests."

The Siamese cat sneers. "Hmmpf, it has to be better than Gypsy's wonder blunder. We still can't use the super-secret cave. All that glitter, I'll never get it all out of my fur." She licks her paw, rubs her ear, and specks of glitter fly in the evening breeze.

The Sphinx speaks up, "As we all know, raccoons are nocturnal. That means they come out at night. We simply turn the night into day."

"Uggh, I take it back, that's crazy. It can't be done. You make Gypsy appear sane," yowls the Siamese.

The Sphinx speaks, "Just hear me out. We place several high intensity lights at the raccoon's favorite dumpster, and when the raccoons come to run their little black paws through the garbage..."

"We blast them with the lights!" bellows Gypsy.

"Blind the raccoons!" squeals Huck.

"Slam the lid!" screeches Finn.

"Lock it!" hollers the Sphinx.

The Siamese rubs her chin. "And the raccoons go out with the morning trash. It just might work."

"Problem solved. It's brilliant. I'm glad I thought of it," bellows Gyspy.

"But, but, it was my idea," complains the Sphinx cat.

"I'm terribly clever!" cries Gypsy.

"Well, it might get rid of the raccoons, but what about the darn unicorn?" asks the Siamese cat.

"Oh, nobody ever catches a unicorn," laughs Huck.

Gypsy rubs her paws together. "Oh, we'll see about that. First, the Totally Ninja Raccoons, and then that troublesome unicorn."

A lightning bug flashes its way across the backyard. Finn notices the insect, and starts to chase it. The other members of the Cat Board remember there are naps to take and mice to chase, and quickly wander into the night.

"This meeting is now over!" yowls Gypsy to the empty darkness. Gypsy remembers she left some food in her dish, and slowly waddles her way back to her house.

"There's a falling star now! Make a wish!"

2

A SHOWER OF STARS

While the wicked Cat Board plots in Wellsboro, the Totally Ninja Raccoons are camping and having fun. The raccoons are watching the stars at Cherry Springs State Park in Potter County.

"So when is this show supposed to start?" asks Kevin.

"I've made popcorn! Extra butter!" shrieks Rascal.

"The Perseid meteor shower is currently at peak activity," explains Bandit.

"Yeah, but when is it scheduled to start?" asks Kevin.

"The shower is ongoing. Even during the day. It's just too bright out to see it then," says Bandit.

"So, you don't know when we'll see a falling star?" challenges Kevin.

"Showers? I thought tonight was supposed to be clear? We'll never see falling stars if it's cloudy and raining," pouts Rascal.

"The best times to view the meteors are between August 9th and August 14th," lectures Bandit.

"In the dark, at night, with no moon," finishes Kevin.

"We are in one of the best places to watch the Perseid meteor showers, here at Cherry Springs," says Bandit.

"Cherry Springs? Yum, that sounds like a great soda, but I'd rather have a cold birch beer," says Rascal.

"No, Cherry Springs State Park is one of the best places for stargazing and the science of astronomy because it's so dark and far away from everything," says Bandit.

"We are almost thirty-three miles from our clubhouse," says Kevin.

"I'm glad we didn't have to walk. I have short legs," explains Rascal.

"Yes, it was kind of our friend the thunderbird to fly us here," says Bandit.

"There's a falling star now! Make a wish!" yelps Kevin.

"I wish I had a nice cold birch beer," says Rascal.

"The proper term for a falling star is a meteor," explains Bandit.

"What do you call one that lands?" asks Kevin.

"That's called a meteorite, but that's a space rock that strikes the planet Earth. They don't land," explains Bandit.

"This one did. It slowed down and landed on the hill behind those trees," says Kevin.

"I saw it, too!" hollers Rascal.

"That is highly unusual. We need to investigate," says Bandit.

"Could we do it tomorrow after a full night's sleep?" asks Kevin.

"And a good breakfast. It's the most important meal of the morning," says Rascal.

"We need to do this now. It could be another evil plan of Gypsy and the Cat Board to take over Wellsboro, then Pennsylvania, and then the world," explains Bandit.

"Could we have a snack first?" asks Rascal.

"Or a nap?" asks Kevin.

"No, we are the Totally Ninja Raccoons and we are..."

Rascal holds up an empty bag. "Totally out of popcorn?"

Kevin gives a big yawn. "Totally tired?"

Bandit puts his paws on his hips. "We are totally going to check this out before morning light. Put on your hiking boots, because we are going on a hike."

"I'm totally sleeping in tomorrow," says Kevin.

"Toast, I'm totally making French toast for breakfast tomorrow," says Rascal.

"What did one slice of bread say to the other slice of bread when he saw some butter and jam on the table?" asks Kevin.

"But bread doesn't talk," says Rascal.

"We're toast! Get it? It's a joke!" laughs

Bandit groans, "Enough bread jokes. They are crumby."

Kevin grins and makes a quip, "I'm on a roll. I come up with the best jokes when you yeast expect it."

"Stop loafing around, and let's get investigating," says Bandit.

"No, it looks like a pattern. It looks like a..."

UNIDENTIFIED FLYING OBJECTS

The Totally Ninja Raccoons hike up the hill. Bandit takes the lead. Kevin stops to scratch his butt, and Rascal takes a break to adjust the straps of his backpack.

"I've been reading the book, *UFOs in Pennsylvania.* Maybe what you saw was a UFO?" says Bandit.

"A UFO? What's that?" asks Kevin.

"I know. I know the answer! It stands for unidentified flying object," whoops Rascal.

"Well, of course it's unidentified. That's why Bandit is dragging us up this hill in the dark," says Kevin.

"UFO is a term created by the United States Air Force to describe any flying object that cannot be identified as a known object," says Bandit.

"A spaceship! He means creatures from another planet!" squeals Rascal.

"Yes, the term is widely used to refer to craft thought to come from outer space," says Bandit.

"Like little green men from Mars!" shouts Rascal.

"Bah, space is cold and dark and empty. You told us about black holes last week. There's no life in space," says Kevin.

"Outer space has more stars than grains of sand on the beaches of Earth, and many of those stars have planets. Maybe it's possible there is life on those planets, just like there is on Earth," says Bandit.

"Like little green men!" exclaims Rascal.

"The movies sometimes show aliens as being little green men from Mars, or even big scary aliens with razor-sharp teeth, or slimy tentacles, but we have no idea what aliens would look like," says Bandit.

"Ha, they would probably be ugly, without fur, like the Sphinx cat on the Cat Board. Maybe she's an alien?" asks Kevin.

"Well, the thing about aliens is that they would be alien, which means strange or foreign, and they could look like anything," says Bandit.

"Like little green men!" exclaims Rascal.

"Well, I guess that is possible, but quite unlikely," says Bandit.

"If there are so many stars, and so many planets, then where are all the aliens?" asks Kevin.

"Are we alone in the universe? That is still an unanswered question," says Bandit.

The Totally Ninja Raccoons come to the top of the hill. There's an open field. The wind gently blows and the grass waves in the night air.

"Well, there's nothing to see here. Let's go back to camp and get some sleep," says Kevin.

"And a snack!" yelps Rascal.

Bandit points. "There, the grass is moving!" he yells.

"Aww, it's just the wind," says Kevin.

Bandit looks closer. "No, it looks like a pattern. It looks like a..."

"Kitty! It looks like a big cat," yells Rascal.

"A really fat cat," says Kevin.

"Maybe it's Gypsy," laughs Rascal.

The grass stops moving. The crickets stop chirping, a bright light shines into the raccoons' eyes, and a loud, deep voice blares out, "TAKE ME TO YOUR LEADER!"

"Why don't you show yourself?"

4

IS BEING GREEN MEAN?

The Ninja Raccoons are totally surprised. Kevin twirls and readies his staff for attack. Bandit draws his sword. Rascal's special glasses turn dark to protect his eyes, and he pulls out his trusty screwdriver.

Bandit throws his shoulders back, stands tall, and announces, "I'm the leader of the Totally Ninja Raccoons."

"I thought I was the leader?" says Kevin.

"Actually, we're really more of a team, and we all have a say," adds Rascal.

"I say we should have stayed at camp," says Kevin.

"I say we should have had s'mores. I love s'mores even more than French toast," reveals Rascal.

The loud, deep voice booms out, "I'm looking for Gypsy, the ruler of Earth, and leader of the Cat Board."

"Oh, I thought you were looking for our leader," says Kevin.

"Are you sure you want to find Gypsy? She isn't very nice," says Rascal.

"Why are you looking for that cruel calico that considers herself a leader of felines?" asks Bandit.

"We are looking for a cute, furry pet. We have been observing Earth. We want kitties!" says the deep, loud voice.

"Uhhh, Gypsy is a full-grown cat, not a kitten, and she is super fat," says Kevin.

"We would like to find Gypsy. And take her back to our planet. Can you help us?" asks the voice.

"Oh, in that case, I do have a map to her super-secret cave in my backpack. I love cartography. That's the study and practice of making maps," says Rascal.

Rascal starts looking through his backpack, and Kevin and Bandit look around the clearing, and try to see the being behind the voice.

"I can't see anyone. Where are you? Why don't you show yourself?"

The deep voice calls out, "Down here!"

"I don't see anything," says Rascal.

"Down here by the kitty!" yells the tiny voice.

"All I see is a pie plate," says Kevin.

"Oh, I love pie!" says Rascal.

"We know!" shout Kevin and Bandit.

"No, we are the pie plate. I mean, that's our ship!" yells the tiny voice.

"It must be a flying saucer. A common shape of a UFO is a flat, silver disc," says Bandit.

"I thought it'd be bigger," says Kevin.

"You're never going to get Gypsy in that," says Rascal.

"Oh, we have a way. Please just place the map by the ship," says the tiny voice.

Rascal places the map by the silver disc. There's a flash of bright light and the map and ship disappear.

"Well, that solves the mystery of the falling star. Let's go get some sleep!" Kevin says, yawning. "All this hiking and cool night air has made me sleepy."

"I could totally go for a nap after breakfast," says Rascal.

"Don't you want to know how the map disappeared and learn more about visitors from another planet?" asks Bandit.

"We should get back to the clubhouse and unpack from our camping trip. I want to finish drawing my map of Cherry Springs State Park," says Rascal.

"Why do you need a map of Cherry Springs? You know where it is," says Bandit.

"I like maps and camping," says Rascal.

"Where do cows go camping?" asks Kevin.

"Cows don't go camping," says Rascal.

"Moo York, get it? It's a camping joke. You could say it was in tents..." laughs Kevin.

Bandit groans. "Kevin, you have to get a better joke book. Let's go back to the clubhouse. I need to read up on aliens."

"Take your positions and get ready for the raccoons."

5

THE TRAP IS SPRUNG

Sleek shadows and one very round, fat shadow creep along a back alley. The members of the Cat Board emerge from the night and gather around a dented dumpster.

Finn, the black cat, gently sniffs the air. "Is that General Tso's Chicken I smell?"

"Don't eat it, Finn, that's the lure. The Ninja Raccoons will smell chicken and climb into the dumpster," says the Sphinx.

"I will set off the flash," says Huck.

"I pull the string," purrs Finn.

"I place this lock on the dumpster," says the Siamese.

"And those pesky raccoons are finally put in their place!" yowls Gypsy.

The Siamese cat rubs her face against the dumpster. "It just may work. Maybe we should have done our own dirty work a long time ago."

"If you want to do something wrong, you have to do it right," says Gypsy.

"With the Totally Ninja Raccoons out of the way, the Cat Board can finally take over Wellsboro, Tioga County, and then the world," says the Siamese cat.

"Yes, the world is mine. I mean, cats will rule and humans will drool," grins Gypsy.

Gypsy motions to the other cats. "Take your positions and let's get ready for those darn raccoons."

"Is it time to eat yet?" asks Finn.

"First, we catch the raccoons, and then we feast," says the Sphinx cat.

"Have you tried this General Tso's Chicken? It's yummy!" says Huck.

"That's for the Totally Ninja Raccoons!" yells the Sphinx.

"Hey, I want some!" whines Finn.

"Everyone, be quiet. I hear something," whispers Gypsy.

The members of the Cat Board crouch down. A humming sound fills the alley. A silver disc glides through the dark, and gently lands in front of the dumpster.

Gypsy waddles up to the object. "Meow, did we get a new dog park? It's nothing but a silly Frisbee."

There's a bright, flashing light, a loud POP, and then silence.

The Sphinx claps her paws together and shouts, "We did it! We captured the Ninja Raccoons!"

The Sphinx smirks and looks around for the other members of the Cat Board, and sees no one. "Fellow members of the Cat Board, let us celebrate. Hello? Where is everyone?"

The silver disc on the ground glows and starts to spin. A booming voice calls out, "Strange, hairless creature! We have what we came for: kitties! They are now ours!"

The small, silver disk rises and shoots down the alley.

"What? My fellow Cat Board friends are gone!" shouts the Sphinx.

"Aliens have catnapped the entire Cat Board!"

6

ASKING FOR HELP

The rusted hulk of a car looms in the dark. A sliver of light reflects off the broken rear view mirror. It's coming from a strange-looking shack in the corner of the junkyard. It's the hidden clubhouse of the Totally Ninja Raccoons. Inside, Bandit reads a book. Kevin swings his staff, and Rascal colors his latest map.

"Those aliens might have been out of this world, but I could have totally taken them," says Kevin.

"Taken them where? Out to dinner?" says Rascal.

"I want to learn more about our alien visitors. I'm reading *War of the Worlds*, by H.G. Wells. It's a fiction book about an alien invasion. I wonder if the aliens we met have a weakness?" says Bandit.

There's a knock at the door.

"Who goes there?" asks Kevin.

"Aliens!" yowls the Sphinx.

"Aliens who?" asks Kevin.

"How many aliens do you know? It's me. The Sphinx, member of the Cat Board!" meows the Sphinx.

"I thought this was supposed to be a secret clubhouse. Only the weird and wacky werewolf knows where it is," says Bandit.

"I might have lost the map to the clubhouse," says Rascal.

"You know where the clubhouse is. Why do you have a map?" asks Kevin.

"I'm a junior cartographer, remember?" replies Rascal.

"Is someone going to answer the door now that the secret is out?" asks Bandit.

Kevin walks across the room and opens the door. A scared Sphinx cat comes rushing into the room, looks around, and slams the door behind her.

"You have to help me. Aliens have catnapped the entire Cat Board!" pleads the Sphinx.

"You are here, and I don't see how this situation is my problem," says Kevin.

"The Cat Board are our fellow Earthlings," says Bandit.

Kevin shakes his head and shivers. "But they sent flying robotic spiders after us, and framed us for the theft of the Wynken, Blynken & Nod statue."

"The Cat Board had Santa Claus kidnapped, and unleashed a wild unicorn on Wellsboro," says Rascal.

"The unicorn dilemma is pretty funny. It really only irritates the members of the Cat Board," laughs Kevin.

"I devised a plan to trap you in a dumpster, but the aliens shrunk the other members of the Cat Board except me, and took off!" exclaims the Sphinx.

"That really isn't convincing me that we should be helping you," says Kevin.

"Because of the Cat Board, we did make new friends like the thunderbird, and Nessie, and we saved Christmas," says Bandit.

"You'll help me save them?" says the Sphinx.

"We've come across these aliens before. We could talk with them and see if we could convince them to change their mind," says Bandit.

"Oh, thank you, thank you, but I have no idea where to find them," says the Sphinx.

"I have an idea of where to start, but it's going to take some help from our friend the thunderbird," says Bandit.

Bandit and Rascal grab their backpacks and get ready to run out the door.

"You're joking, right?" asks Kevin.

"Actually, that reminds me of a joke," says Rascal.

"You don't know any jokes," says Kevin.

"Sure I do! What did the aliens say to the Cat Board?" asks Rascal.

"Take me to your litter!" answers Kevin.

"Stop joking around, you two. We have a ninja job to do," says Bandit.

"I never get to say the punch lines," pouts Rascal as he puts his colored pencils into his backpack.

"We don't call them little green men for nothing,"

7

SPRING TO ACTION

It's a clear night. The stars are bright, and the Totally Ninja Raccoons are back at Cherry Springs State Park with the Sphinx cat.

"We talked to the aliens near here when we were watching the Perseid meteor shower," explains Bandit.

"What did they look like? I didn't see them when they catnapped my fellow Cat Board members," says the Sphinx cat.

"We didn't actually see what they looked like, but we had some great snacks," says Rascal.

"And we did see the spaceship land!" exclaims Kevin.

"I always thought the universe was bigger than cats. There is so much more to conquer once we get done with Earth," says the Sphinx cat.

"Do you want our help or not?" asks Bandit.

The Totally Ninja Raccoons and the nearly hairless Sphinx hike to where the Raccoons first saw the aliens and the drawing of the cat.

"Is that supposed to be a cat? It's sooo fat," says the Sphinx.

"Gypsy is fat!" exclaims Kevin.

"Well, it's hard to disagree with that, but she prefers to be called fluffy," says the Sphinx.

"I'm fluffy too, and I have little legs," says Rascal.

Bandit points towards the cat drawing. "There! Near the tail of the fat cat, it's the space ship!"

"It's so small! I thought it'd be bigger," says the Sphinx.

"We don't call them little green men for nothing," says Kevin.

"Are they actually green?" asks the Sphinx.

"We haven't actually seen them yet. We've only heard them," replies Rascal.

"Aliens, we would like to speak with you," requests Bandit.

"Hello, big, furry, masked creatures. We are pleased to see you again. We wish to thank you for the information that led us to the Cat Board," says the alien voice.

"Meow! You helped them???" asks the Sphinx.

"I was just being helpful, and they wanted to know a good place to eat," replies Rascal.

"We'd like you to let the members of the Cat Board go. They belong on Earth, and they don't want to leave their home," says Bandit.

"We came to Earth for kitties! We've seen videos on the Internet with cute kittens and we just had to have some," says the alien voice.

"They are my friends! Please let them go!" pleads the Sphinx cat.

"We didn't come across the galaxy to go home without a souvenir," says the alien voice.

"We could help you find something else to replace the kitties," says Bandit.

"How about a postcard? I have a postcard in here somewhere," says Rascal as he rummages around in his backpack.

"We want something small and furry," says the alien voice.

"How about a Woolly Bear Caterpillar? It's small, fuzzy, and even has 'cat' in there," says Kevin.

"Well, does it do anything?" asks the alien voice.

"It changes into a moth," says Bandit.

"And forecasts the winter weather," says Rascal.

"That's just folklore," says Kevin.

"So, this caterpillar is magic?" asks the alien voice.

"No, it's the larva form of a species," replies Bandit.

"I do know of a magical creature that would be great. It has hair, hooves, a horn, and it's magical. It also smells delightful," says the Sphinx.

"That sounds like a suitable replacement. What is this magical creature called?" asks the alien voice.

"It's called a unicorn. You'll love it!" meows the Sphinx.

"Where can we find this unicorn?" ask the aliens.

"It's on the map I gave you. It lives in Gypsy's Cave," says Rascal.

"We must have this magical creature. Here, take back these cats. They are no longer sufficient for our needs. We no longer want them," say the aliens.

A tiny landing ramp emerges from the space ship. Tiny creatures walk down the ramp carrying a box. Inside the box is the entire Cat Board. They are tiny!

"See, they really are little green men, and they have purple polka dots!" yells Rascal.

"One of them has pink polka dots," says Kevin.

"My friends, they are so tiny!" yowls the Sphinx cat.

"Yes, we had to shrink them to make them fit on our ship, but that will wear off in 1000 chronos," say the aliens.

"That's going to be forever," cries Finn.

"Oh, that equals about 2.457 of your Earth hours," replies the little green man.

"Get me out of this box!" yowls Gypsy.

"I thought cats liked boxes," snickers Kevin.

"Goodbye, huge Earthlings. We will retrieve this unicorn and take it back to our home planet," say the little green men.

The flying saucer softly glows, rises, and quickly disappears.

"Can we go home now?" asks Kevin.

"Our job here is done," says Bandit.

"Don't forget me! I have tiny legs and I don't know where I am!" cries Gypsy.

"Would you like a map?" asks Rascal.

"I'll never make it back to my cave. Meow, I mean the Cat Board is a long way from home. We have plots to plan. We need a ride!" cries Gypsy.

"It's not that far back. It's nothing compared to the vastness of the universe," says Bandit.

"I wonder if the little green men will make it back to their planet?" asks Kevin.

"Wow, what would it be like to map the stars?" wonders Rascal.

"You're going to need a LOT more paper," laughs Kevin.

"And more colored pencils," replies Rascal.

"What is that sweet, sickly smell?"

WHAT DO
UNICORNS EAT?

The little green men with the purple polka dots sit at the console of their tiny silver spaceship, flying through the darkness of outer space.

"I can't wait to get home so we can show everyone our new pet," says the little green man with the purple polka dots.

"What did that giant, hairless beast call it again?" asks the little green man with the pink polka dots.

"A unicorn," says the purple polka dot alien.

"We are going to be famous," says the pink polka dot man.

"What does a unicorn eat?" says the purple polka dot man.

"Berries? Corn? Lucky Charms? I didn't think to ask," says the pink polka dot man.

"What is that sweet, sickly smell?" asks the purple polka dot man.

"I don't know! What is this sparkly, shiny stuff all over the control board?" asks the pink polka dot man.

There's a quiet sound from the back of the spaceship. It sounds like a mix of a horse's neigh and a snicker.

"What was that? Did you lock that beast's cage?" asks the purple polka dot man.

"Don't be foolish! Of course I did. Where are we? I don't recognize this region of space. The instruments don't seem to work with all this glitter!" yells the pink polka dot man.

"I think maybe we should have gone with the caterpillar," says the purple polka dot man.

"I think we are lost in space!" yells the pink polka dot man.

Laughter echoes through the spaceship followed by silence.

THE END?

What do you think happens to the Little Green Men? You can write the author and tell him what you think happens next...

Cherry Springs State Park

Cherry Springs State Park is located in Potter County, Pennsylvania. It is named for a large stand of Black Cherry trees in the park. The park is popular with stargazers and astronomers due to its exceptionally dark skies. It is one of the best places in the eastern United States for watching stars.

Cherry Springs State Park was named Pennsylvania's first dark sky park in 2000. The park hosts several star parties a year. There are regular stargazing and educational programs for the public at the park.

Cherry Springs also offers trails for hiking, biking, and snowmobiling, and offers camping and picnic facilities. The surrounding state forest is home to a variety of plants and animals. Contact the State Park office for facility seasons and hours.
Phone: 814-435-1037

OBSERVATORY

CHERRY SPRINGS STATE PARK

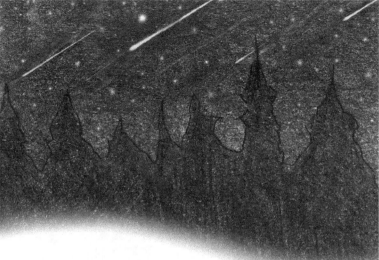

Perseid Meteor Shower

The Perseid meteor shower happens every August. The shower occurs in the Northern Hemisphere from July 23 through August 23. The date of maximum visibility is usually August 11 to the 13th. The Perseids are named after the constellation of Perseus. You might be able to see up to 100 meteors per hour!

The Perseids are pea-sized bits of rocky debris that come from the comet Swift-Tuttle. The comet is slowly falling apart as it orbits our sun. The Earth's path around the Sun carries us through this comet debris every mid-August.

The particles are called metoroids. When one of these metoroids hits the Earth's atompshere, it creates a white-hot streak of super-heated air and creates a meteor, also known as a falling star. Almost none hit the ground, but if one does, it is called a meteorite.

The Little Green Men

The universe is a very big place. It is so huge that it is difficult to understand just how enormous it is. Humans have always wondered if we are alone in the universe. The universe is filled with stars. Many of those stars have planets, and some of those planets may contain life, or aliens.

The word 'alien' is a popular word for a being from another planet. We don't know if there is life on other planets. Some scientists think that is possible. The branch of biology concerned with life from other planets is called exobiology or astrobiology.

Some people claim they have seen aliens, but science hasn't been able to prove it, at least not yet. What do you think aliens look like? Would they be gray? Green? Scaly? Slimy? Do aliens even exist? Are we alone in the universe? Stay curious, become a reading ninja, and decide for yourself!

About the Author

Kevin resides in Wellsboro, just a short hike from the Pennsylvania Grand Canyon. When he's not writing, you can find him at *From My Shelf Books & Gifts*, an independent bookstore he runs with his lovely wife, several helpful employees, and two friendly cats, Huck & Finn.

He's recently become an honorary member of the Cat Board, and when he's not scooping the litter box, or feeding Gypsy her tuna, he's writing more stories about the Totally Ninja Raccoons. Be sure to catch their next big adventure, *The Totally Ninja Raccoons Meet the Jersey Devil*.

You can write him at:

From My Shelf Books & Gifts
7 East Ave., Suite 101
Wellsboro, PA 16901

www.wellsborobookstore.com

About the Illustrator

Jubal Lee is a former Wellsboro resident who now resides in sunny Florida, due to his extreme allergic reaction to cold weather.

He is an eclectic artist who, when not drawing raccoons, thunderbirds, and the like, enjoys writing, bicycling, and short walks on the beach.

THE
TOTALLY NINJA
RACCOONS
MEET BIGFOOT

by Kevin Coolidge

THE
TOTALLY NINJA
RACCOONS
MEET THE
WEIRD &
WACKY
WEREWOLF

by Kevin Coolidge

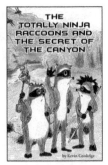

THE
TOTALLY NINJA
RACCOONS AND
THE SECRET OF
THE CANYON

by Kevin Coolidge

THE
TOTALLY NINJA
RACCOONS
MEET THE
THUNDERBIRD

by Kevin Coolidge

THE
TOTALLY NINJA
RACCOONS AND
THE CATMAS CAPER

THE TOTALLY
NINJA RACCOONS
AND THE SECRET OF
NESSMUK LAKE

by Kevin Coolidge

THE TOTALLY
NINJA RACCOONS
MEET THE LITTLE
GREEN MEN

by Kevin Coolidge

Get your own copies of the adventures with the Totally Ninja Raccoons!

The Totally Ninja Raccoons Meet Bigfoot

_____ copies @ $5.99 each = _____

The Totally Ninja Raccoons Meet the Weird & Wacky Werewolf

_____ copies @ $5.99 each = _____

The Totally Ninja Raccoons and the Secret of the Canyon

_____ copies @ $5.99 each = _____

The Totally Ninja Raccoons Meet the Thunderbird

_____ copies @ $5.99 each = _____

The Totally Ninja Raccoons and the Catmas Caper

_____ copies @ $6.99 each = _____

The Totally Ninja Raccoons and the Secret of Nessmuk Lake

_____ copies @ $6.99 each = _____

The Totally Ninja Raccoons Meet the Little Green Men

_____ copies @ $6.99 each = _____

Subtotal = _____

$2.99 shipping = _____
(15 books or less)

Total Enclosed = _____

Send this form, with payment via check or money order, to:
From My Shelf Books & Gifts
7 East Ave., Suite 101
Wellsboro, PA 16901

or call **(570) 724-5793**
Also available at **wellsborobookstore.com**

9 781641 364348